THEY SAID THAT HE WOULD NEVER GO FAR BUT HE DID

A SHORT STORY ABOUT OVERCOMING LIFE'S ADVERSITIES

DWAYNE JANSZ

They Said That He Would Never Go Far But He Did.

Dwayne Jansz.

Dwayne Jansz.
dwayne.98@live.com.

THEY SAID THAT HE
WOULD NEVER GO FAR
BUT HE DID

CONTENTS

PROLOGUE

John is a 17-year-old boy who is failing in school. Initially, the reason for his numerous failed attempts at virtually everything he does seems to be a mystery to those around him. As a result of this, John comes across as being enigmatic to those who don't know him. Then, he develops a deep inner depression which eventually manifests itself outwardly. When the root cause is found out, it changes the course of events in John's life. John is going through something that many people go through in life. However, despite all odds something spectacular occurs.

You have power over your mind - not outside events. Realize this, and you will find strength.

-Marcus Aurelius (121 AD - 180 AD)

There once was a boy who thought that he could repress his feelings forever. Little did he know that his feelings would eventually get the best of him, and eventually take over until he decided to take control of his life through his own choices, decisions and actions.

Chapter 1

A Briefing

Hardship concomitantly with turmoil is what builds people and helps them garner a wealth of knowledge together with experience.

It's 6am on a bright sunny morning, but John is very hesitant to get out of bed. Unfortunately, he doesn't have an option. It's a school day and John feels a sense of dread. As John coerces himself out of bed, he feels unwell due to the high amount of adrenaline in his bloodstream. John feels his heart pounding in his chest and he attributes it to be due to the stress and anxiety that he's experiencing. Somatically, something sinister seems to be going on with John. However, to John, this routine is normality.

"John, are you ready for school?" asks mom.

"I'm getting ready," says John in a monotonous tone after his morning shower. John tries hard to repress his emotions and he tries not to burst out into tears. And John succeeds.

Little do John's parents know of the inner turmoil that John is going through on an emotional level. John is being bullied at school. The bullying that John is enduring at school is having a massive and profound impact on his subconscious mind in a very dreadful way. Moreover, the bullying is affecting John's emotional well-being in a very negative and undesirable way. But John has learned to repress his emotions, just to please everyone around him and despite all odds, John continues to act normal outwardly since he feels that this is probably the best coping mechanism to deal with his problems.

John arrives at school at 7:45am anxious and nervous of what the day may hold. John ponders whether it'll be just like yesterday and whether he would have to endure being tormented and harassed again.

As John walks through the corridor to his class room, someone slaps him violently on his head. The blow to John's head feels profound, almost as if his skull is fractured. Instantaneously, John experiences a burst of adrenaline due to extreme emotional shock. John has become unusually fearful of retorting back and standing up for himself, since the bullying has affected his self-confidence and self-esteem so badly that he now feels he doesn't stand a chance against the bullies. John doesn't even know who slapped him as he's in shark infested waters and he has come to comprehend that suppositions make bad endings. Moreover, there is no evidence since everyone has turned against him and the school cameras are malfunctional. Therefore, John makes up his mind to pretend it never happened, forget about it and act as if he feels fine. John hopes in desperation that he will never get slapped again and prays that it is the last incident he will ever face.

John doesn't trust anyone either, as he feels that at this point in time, trusting someone is the most complicated thing, it's like hoping a pebble will never get kicked.

Before you know it, the day is over. John tries desperately to forget about the aggressiveness that he has encountered during school hours by the bullies. Being a meek mannered and highly considerate individual who has off the chart emotional intelligence, John finds it difficult to be assertive and dominant when required, since he intuitively feels that he may hurt his opponent's feelings despite all odds. A lack of self-confidence and assertiveness seems to be contributing to and increasing John's susceptibility to being bullied as well. Therefore, John feels helpless when someone bullies him directly, indirectly, verbally, physically or even emotionally. Moreover, retorting back to the bully makes him feel bad since John tends to be a very compassionate young man and he feels that the bully may be mentally ill. With all of this going on, John feels horrendously victimized.

Mom arrives to pick John up from school.

"How was school darling?" asks mom exuberantly and enthusiastically since she's clueless as to what life is like from John's perspective.

"Oh, everything was absolutely fine," says John showing outward cheerfulness. However, on the contrary, deep down within, John is suffering unbearably.

As John lay in bed for the night, he recalls the events of the day. Right now, John's mind is like a tape recorder. John's mind is vividly replaying the past events of the day that he recollects with phenomenal accuracy, and crystal-clear clarity. John's mind seems to be racing with the thoughts of the day like a formula one race car racing through the race tracks of a racing circuit at full speed. Moreover, John is literally reliving the day once again in his mind and he can even feel the powerful emotions he felt whilst at school earlier in the day as well. This is another contributive factor which is affecting

John's psychological and physiological well-being since he has developed some sort of stress as a consequence of getting bullied.

John hears the bullies saying vividly:

"You'll never amount to anything John."

"You'll never get far in life John."

"You're worthless and not worth a dime John."

John doesn't recollect learning anything at school, he just remembers being insulted, bullied, tormented and harassed. John ponders to himself whether he would be better off dead if life is going to continue like this for him.

"I'm better off dead," John murmurs to himself whilst he lay in bed for the night.

It's impossible for anyone to concentrate and put their mind on something when they are in a toxic environment since their focus tends to be concentrated on the problem that their facing, hence, this brings about even more difficulties. John is no different since he is young and still has a lot to learn in life. Therefore, John is yet to understand that if he were to always put his focus and energy on a problem, he'll just jeopardize everything by adding fuel to the fire.

John is undergoing a tremendous amount of stress and by not telling anyone, matters seem to be just getting worse by the day. John innately feels that things are on a download spiral and he knows this more than anyone since he's naturally gifted and he possesses a strong sense of intuition.

"I wonder what to do," John says silently to himself whilst lying in bed as he simultaneously sighs. Then John starts sobbing uncontrollably since he feels sorry for himself. John's bed is like a sea of tears now.

John is at a very dark time in his life where he cannot see the light at the end of the tunnel.

John is pondering whether everyone goes through bullying and feels suicidal at some point in their life or he wonders whether he is the only one. John then goes on to ponder as to whether all what he is experiencing is a normal phenomenon. After all, John has witnessed the bullies attacking other innocent civilians and individuals at school as well. This leads John to conclude that since he isn't the only one been bullied, there cannot be an ulterior motive of the bullies, since this was his initial suspicion. At the start, John felt that he was being bullied because people were envious of him, but now he concludes that this was just a false assumption of his based upon a false premise.

John decides to forget about the past and try and move on enthusiastically despite all odds. John really hopes that things will change for the better soon and that a miracle will hopefully take place as well.

Due to the immense amount of stress that John is going through, John has become an insomniac as well. However, John eventually falls asleep at 2am.

Chapter 2

Trying To Cope

Our choices, decisions and actions, whether positive or negative tend to mould our life into what it eventually becomes. The good thing about this is that we can always make amendments and modifications by changing our perspectives and ways of thinking.

Initially very virtuous, John has now developed a myriad of unhealthy coping mechanisms as a way to deal with the unwanted stress he's experiencing at school. John has discovered an undesirable way to ease the pain and suffering. John resorts to watching countless hours of TV and binge eating after school. John is resorting to these undesirable measures daily and they are having a detrimental and profound negative impact on his overall health. Moreover, it acts as a way to distract John's mind from thinking about the unpleasantness of being bullied, thus, it seems to be reinforcing the continuation of the behavior. As a result of all of this, John is being and feeling very unproductive. And John feels drained energetically on an emotional level as well. On the other hand, his healthy peers are out socializing, exercising and playing sports. John's healthy peers are having fun and enjoying life, whilst John has isolated himself in his house. Moreover, the bullying has prompted him to take refuge in his bedroom after school. Although John does indeed feel confined, he doesn't mind it, at least he's in his comfort zone and he doesn't have to deal with uncomfortable feelings.

But one day, something changed.

"Something doesn't feel right about this. I need to make a change in my life. I'm going to stop this and start exercising with my dogs for a start," John thinks to himself.

John knows that it is not relevant to being bullied at school, however, he decides to start making amendments in his personal life with the intention and hope of bolstering his overall success in life. Internally, John feels that doing anything considered to be positive by society will help him succeed down the line. Therefore, John is in the midst of thinking futuristically which will prove to be very beneficial for John, especially down-the-line.

John starts by going for a walk with his dogs every evening. John finds it a good way to deal with stress and he feels optimistically confident about his decision. Moreover, John feels it's good to be outside and breath in some fresh air. After the evening walk with his dogs, John feels energized and rejuvenated after a hard day's work of never ending school assignments. However, he has socially isolated himself for quite a sustained period of time, therefore, John will need to relearn and mentally grasp how to be socially adept again.

Walking the dogs, playing with them and interacting with them is aiding John in distracting his mind from stressful thoughts. As a result of this, John has discovered a new form of a recreational activity that he can look forward to daily with sheer optimism and unmitigated enthusiasm. Moreover, it clearly seems to be putting John on the correct path to success.

Exercise in any form is good for everyone and John is beginning to realize this more than ever now as time goes on. John has begun the process of reinitiating socialization with the outside world and has reached a milestone from one aspect in his life.

Chapter 3

A Downward Spiral

What you go through is what will eventually make you and help you.

Despite John trying earnestly to improve his life all by himself, he has come in for a nervous breakdown. John seems to be anxious and severely depressed. John's parents realize and come to terms that medical intervention is imperative in their son's case. John's parents are finally able to comprehend the severity of the problem and they are also now aware that time is of the essence since it is widely known that suicide ultimately follows depression.

John is taken for medical treatment to Prof. Dr. TM, so that John can be thoroughly evaluated.

"John, it seems like you're going through a lot. I've spoken to your parents and you're going to be homeschooled online since your suffering from the stress of being bullied, therefore, a temporary change of environment will allow your health to recuperate," says Prof. Dr. TM in a compassionate and sympathetic tone.

Prof. Dr. TM continues, "You'll be fine in no time, but I'll have to do some work with you."

John undergoes treatment with Prof. Dr. TM for about 2 months, and John walks out absolutely fine at the end. John feels miraculously healed from every aspect. John is now on the long road to recovery and he himself knows that it's not going to be easy, since success requires consistent and dedicated work. But John knows the pain is definitely worth the success waiting for him at the finish line. Therefore, John decides to continue the hobbies and recreational activities that he created earlier, such as exercising with his dogs.

So now, John is homeschooled online with a reputable and local government and internationally approved online school. The online school is a replica to a brick-and-mortar school, the only difference is that the work is done online. Although the online school does have an academy where you could go to anytime in the week, John prefers not to as he feels children his age are very immature in many aspects. John is thankful, as he is now able to reflect on his life. Moreover, he can find ways to improve his life by himself so that he will be set for a successful future. Lastly, although there is quite a lot of work from John's online school and it's the exact replica of a brick-and-mortar school, the fact that bullying has decreased substantially and that he has been removed from the toxic environment he was once in, it allows for a much needed and beneficial deep self-introspection.

During this period in time, John even meditates for answers that will help bolster his quality of life. It also allows John to garner ideas about self-improvement as well. John has also begun a daily habit of reading self-help books by world-renowned and internationally acclaimed authors as well. John now feels that he is beginning to get in control of his fate and destiny. This in turn acts as a confidence bolster to increase John's self-esteem, especially in social situations which he had many deficits in initially. Moreover, John has finally come to realize and comprehend that we always have a choice and that we always have control of our life!

Chapter 4

Moving On With Life

Move forth with optimistic confidence, not backward remorse or regret. The only time you should look back and ponder on your life in retrospect is to learn from your mistakes.

Currently, John's days are filled with happiness and joy. A myriad of things are gradually and steadily improving in his life. John now seems to be able to see the light at the end of the dark and misty tunnel. Moreover, life seems to be a lot brighter from

John's perspective now. It's a bit like a bad time period has passed. John is now left with a wealth of experience that he could potentially utilize to help him prosper throughout his life.

It's 6am. And John is up for his morning walk with his dogs. No more heart thumping adrenaline is released into his bloodstream. John feels enthusiastically ecstatic and optimistically confident about the day ahead. Moreover, John feels as if everything seems to be gradually reverting back to normalcy. On the walk with his dogs, John is able to confidently converse now with strangers, thus, his fear and bad connection with his peers at his previous school due to being bullied is slowly diminishing.

John's confidence has shot up after changing his mindset and outlook on everything. John plays with his dogs in the garden after he arrives back home after the morning walk and this provides him with an imminent burst of dopamine. John feels like he is on top of the world. And John feels invincible, like a superhero, which is going to propel him to reach even greater heights along his current path.

In no time, John is on his MacBook Pro to log onto his virtual high school platform. John continues working throughout the day on his school work. Although done online, it's a typical school day for John. And the work consists of assignments, tests, quizzes, and essays on various subjects such as Biology, Chemistry, Physics, Trigonometry, Pre-calculus, Latin, History and so on. It is definitely not easy, no two ways about it, but John knows that hard work always pays off in the end.

After John's school day is over, he reads the local newspaper and comes across something intriguing: A dog show that judges' dogs purely on conformation and morphology is coming up in several months time. An idea pops up in John's head and John, now an A* student, decides to work with his dogs for the upcoming dog show with the hope of winning a prize. Just the visualization of winning self-motivates John to go for it eagerly.

Fast forward to the official date of the dog show.

John arrives at the area where the dog show is going to be held. John arrives on time and he observes many people at the dog show with their dogs, however, John is more than sure that both of his dogs are exceptional and that they will definitely win. John is confident about his much-anticipated success.

Fast forward to the final results of the dog show by the specialist dog breed conformation and morphology judge: John wins with either of his dogs at the conformation and morphology show and is awarded best of breed for both of his dogs. John feels proud of himself and his dogs. John worked with both of his dogs together for months on end in preparation for the dog show and winning it has proved his effort to be worthy and commendable. John's rugged, determined hard work and persevering nature to succeed has paid off in a stupendous manner.

John has learned a valuable lesson from his experience at the dog show: Dreams cause visualizations to eventually materialize.

John hears that words and ideas are being passed around in the society and community where he lives. The words are passed amongst John's former friends, his relatives and his family members as well.

"How on earth did John manage to train his dogs all by himself? After all, he never amounted to much back in the day," says one person in utter dismay at the positive and profound change in John from someone who was depressed due to being bullied to someone who now seems to be at the very beginning of climbing the ladder to success and greatness.

"Remember the way John was, keep that idea in mind and just look at him now! I wonder what else John will be able to achieve and accomplish in his life. At this rate, John may very well be one of the world's most successful and influential people somewhere down the line," says someone else in consternation and utter astonishment at John's drastic change from a depressed human-being to a completely normal, healthy and strong individual.

"I always thought he would be a patient and amount to nothing," says another in outrageous shock at John's positive progress.

"If John's like this now, he'll be a million times more successful by the time he's 25 years than I'll be at 50 years," says yet another individual so surprised that he is having a tough time comprehending John's positive and desirable change.

Apparently, as time goes on, things are only beginning to drastically and profoundly change for the better for John.

John eventually graduates from high school with flying colors. The graduation ceremony is held at a world class hotel. Therefore, it was a grand event. Moreover, John has been on the honor roll numerous times whilst in high school. At the graduation ceremony John is also the valedictorian. John feels very proud of himself and his accomplishments as well. On a separate side note, John intuitively feels that his pet dogs and guinea pigs have aided him on his journey as he shares a passion for dogs and has always had from a very young age.

Things seem to be working out very well for John. Prudently, John realizes that resilience and hard work ultimately pay off. Therefore, John decides to continue doing what he's doing despite any adversity. It's like John has been awarded a miraculous new life by the universe. John feels that he is now in full control of his life, this in turn acts as a motivator to bolster his self-confidence which is essential for anyone to succeed in life.

Chapter 5

Success

And when you succeed the whole world will look at you with awe, for they did not know that you had the innate potential within you to succeed for it laid dormant all this time.

Times flies and before you know it John is awarded a scholarship at a prestigious university for his bachelor's degree. It is just the very beginning of what will later on prove to be a very successful and awe-inspiring career for John. John is destined for greatness.

People are shocked now. A boy they felt would be worthless and would be a nobody in life, now seems to be turning into someone exceptional. And this someone, isn't ordinary, but rather seems to be an exceptionally talented and gifted human being who has the innate potential of raising the vibrations of humanity itself.

As time moves on John's success and accomplishments are increasing gradually and steadily.

Fast forward to 20 years later.

John is a multi-millionaire. Apart from being a brilliant veterinarian, John has several passive sources of income. Moreover, he has a flying license to fly both private and commercial jets. John is living the high life now, and he donates regularly to charities and helps uplift people stuck in poverty as well.

And what about those who ridiculed John, humiliated him and felt he would never get far in life, or amount to anything? Well, success spoke for itself for John. The bullies who bullied John never got far in life themselves. Many of the bullies got stuck in a rut and eventually resorted to suicide, but others got stuck in the 9-5 trap and never really achieved much in their life. However, many of the bullies ended up homeless. But John, on the other hand, was so rich he could have and afford anything most people could only dream of, such as a mansion or a Ferrari with ease.

Despite all odds and no one believing in John, he rose to great heights and so can you.

We are all deserving of greatness in life and in everything that we do.

People will ridicule you and humiliate you, but what goes around eventually comes around. And of course, justice always prevails.

We all have the power and ability within us to evolve into great beings no matter how difficult things may seem!

EPILOGUE

Despite all odds, despite the hardship, the criticism endured and the bullying faced anyone has the innate potential to reach great heights and do something meaningful in their life. And so, this was the case with John who little knew his difficult past would evolve into a stellar future.

ACKNOWLEDGEMENTS

Thank you to every soul who has had a positive impact on me. A special thanks to my parents and brother who've always been very supportive in rough times. Thank you to Tyson, Cooper, Molly, Snowie(RIP May 2014- October 2018) and Abby my beloved, amicable and docile pets for teaching me about the importance of being jovial against all odds in rough times.

AUTHOR'S NOTE

I decided to write a book that depicts what one boy went through on his journey that many people have experienced in life, "bullying."

A lot of people often times don't even realize that they are being bullied in the first place since it can be so subtle in certain cases. On the other hand, it can be so profound that the person being bullied may resort to suicide as a way to end their pain and suffering if the turmoil endured becomes unbearable. But all in all, bullying can have a massive negative impact on the person being bullied even if the person being bullied doesn't fully comprehend it. However, the ending doesn't always have to be disheartening and tragic.

Success is possible despite hardship!

A Note About the Author

Dwayne Jansz is a high school graduate who was on the honor roll twice whilst in high school. Moreover, he holds a diploma in psychology. He decided to write this book in his free time with the hope of helping people who read it by offering them what has aided him on his own path in life. Lastly, he loves animals and enjoys gardening in his spare time.

They Said That He Would Never Go Far But He Did.

Dwayne Jansz.

Dwayne Jansz
dwayne.98@live.com

Things happen, but we can choose to decide how we allow it to affect us.

Printed in Great Britain
by Amazon